MOLLY OF DENALI™

A-maze-ing Snow

Based on a television episode
written by Douglas Wood

HARPER

An Imprint of HarperCollins*Publishers*

Copyright © 2019 WGBH Educational Foundation
The PBS KIDS logo is a registered trademark of Public Broadcasting Service and used with permission.

MOLLY OF DENALI™ is produced by WGBH Kids and Atomic Cartoons in association with CBC Kids.

Funding for MOLLY OF DENALI is provided by the Corporation for Public Broadcasting and by public television viewers. In addition, the contents of MOLLY OF DENALI were developed under a grant from the Department of Education. However, those contents do not necessarily represent the policy of the Department of Education, and you should not assume endorsement by the Federal Government. The project is funded by a Ready To Learn grant (PR/AWARD No. U295A150003, CFDA No. 84.295A).

Manufactured in China.
ISBN 978-0-06-295038-3
Typography by Brenda E. Angelilli
19 20 21 22 23 SCP 10 9 8 7 6 5 4 3 2 1

Hey, everyone! It's me, Molly! And my friends Tooey and Trini. We live in Qyah, Alaska.

Last night there was a HUGE blizzard. School's closed today, so my friends and I are playing basketball. And I'm taking video!

Tooey tries to block Trini from shooting the basketball.
When Trini makes her shot, the ball goes up through the net
backward and lands on the roof of the school! Oh no!

KA-BOOM!

Suddenly, the school roof caves in!

"Did I just break the roof?" Trini asks.

"It broke from the weight of all the snow," I say.

"Let's go tell someone," says Tooey.

We go to the Tribal Hall and tell everyone what happened.
There's a hole in the school roof and no money to fix it. We have to
come up with some cash or this snow day turns into a snow year!

"Let's have a carnival!" I suggest. "With all sorts of carnival-y stuff, like snowshoe races, fiddling, and hot chocolate!"

"And a blanket toss contest!" says Trini. The blanket toss is a traditional Iñupiat game.

Everyone loves the idea. This fundraiser will be a fun-raiser!

Everyone has a lot of work to do to get ready for the carnival.

My mom is setting up a moose chili cook-off! My grandpa is polishing the trophy for the blanket toss. All this snow gives me an idea...

"Let's make a snow maze!" I say to Tooey.

"I like it!" Tooey says.

"Let's start building," I say. I'm excited to get started.

"You can't just build a maze," says Tooey. "We need a plan first. Let's draw out a map of what we want the maze to look like."

Back at my house, Tooey works on drawing the map
while I research famous mazes.
  "Look at this one!" I say, showing Tooey my computer.
"It's got twists and turns and dead ends."

"And check this one out!" I say. "It's the world's largest snow maze, in Poland. It has high walls so you can't see where you are." Tooey quickly adds all our great ideas to the map. This is going to be the best snow maze ever!

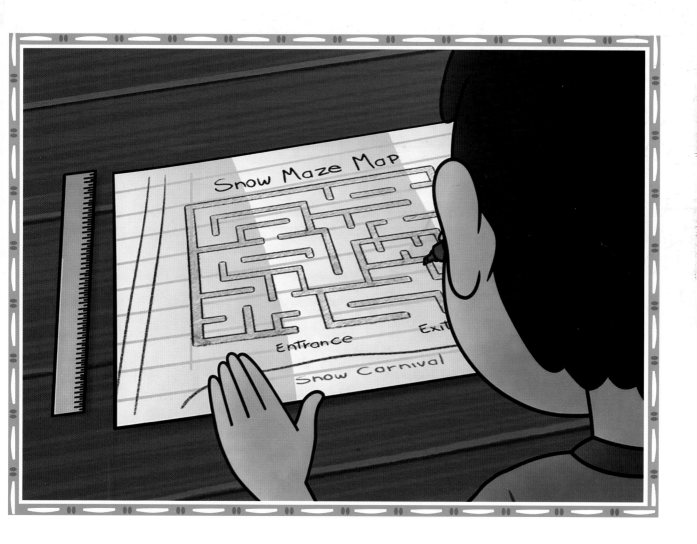

After we have finished our map, it's time to build the maze. Good thing our town has a snowplow! We use walkie-talkies to communicate.

"Okay, boss, tell me where to turn," says my dad. Tooey and I consult the map.

Dad turns left and . . . **CLUNK!**

We've got a problem . . . There's a big rock in the way of where one of our paths is supposed to be!

"My map is all wrong now! The rock is in the way of all these paths," says Tooey.

"Don't worry," I say. "We can fix the map later."

Dad moves his snowplow around the rock so we can keep building the maze. When we finally finish, the maze looks fantastic!

"Now let's go warm up with some hot chocolate!" I say.

It's carnival day! Everyone is ready for fiddling and jig dancing, the blanket toss contest, and especially our amazing maze! My dog, Suki, helps Tooey and me watch our station.

"Quyana!" Tooey says to our maze customers, which means thank you in the Yup'ik language. "Enjoy the maze!"

"Maze time!" Trini says, coming up to us.

"I thought you wanted to do the blanket toss," I say.

"This will only take ten minutes. I'm great at mazes!" Trini says.

My dad agrees to watch the maze, so Tooey and I get to explore the rest of the carnival. There's so much to see!

When we get back to the maze, we hear a shout.

"Help!" Trini yells from inside the maze. "I can't find my way out!"

"We'll get you out," Tooey says. "Stay where you are!"

Tooey enters the maze. "Trini!" he calls.

"Tooey!" she calls back.

Tooey uses his map and the sound of Trini's voice to find her.

"Yay! Let's get out of here. The blanket toss is starting!" Trini says.

Tooey looks at the map again. There's a dead end where a path should be.

"Uh oh!" Tooey says.

We forgot to fix the map after that rock got in the way! I need to think fast. Just then, I get an idea. Suki can find anything!

"Tooey, call Suki's name!" I yell from outside the maze.

"SUKI!" Tooey calls. Suki bolts into the maze.

Suki finds Tooey and Trini right away. Tooey and
Trini hug and pat Suki.
"Good dog! Lead the way back, girl!" Tooey says.
Suki turns and runs back through the maze.
Tooey and Trini run after her.

They are about to announce the winner of the
blanket toss contest when we run over.

"Can I have a turn? Please?" Trini asks.

"Of course, young lady." My grandpa lifts Trini onto the blanket. The blanket holders toss Trini high into the air. This tradition was first used so hunters could see a long distance to find animals. Now people do it for fun, to see who can be tossed the highest!

The carnival was a huge success! Trini won the blanket toss contest. And thanks to our Qyah community, we already have enough money to start fixing the school roof. Speaking of fixing things, we fixed the map, too. The snow maze won't melt for at least a month. Now we can find someone if they get lost again!

Best of all, for now we're holding school at my family's trading post!